The Emperor's New Clothes

Graphic Spin is published by Stone Arch Books
151 Good Counsel Drive, P.O. Box 669
Mankato, Minnesota 56002
www.stonearchbooks.com

Library of Congress Cataloging-in-Publication Data

Peters, Stephanie True, 1965-
 The Emperor's new clothes : the graphic novel / by Hans Christian Andersen ;
retold by Stephanie Peters ; illustrated by Jeffrey Stewart Timmins.
   p. cm. -- (Graphic spin)
 ISBN 978-1-4342-1595-6 (lib. bdg.) -- ISBN 978-1-4342-1744-8 (pbk.)
1. Graphic novels. [1. Graphic novels. 2. Fairy tales.] I. Timmins, Jeffrey Stewart,
ill. II. Andersen, H. C. (Hans Christian), 1805-1875. Kejserens nye klæder. III.
Title.
 PZ7.7.P44Em 2010
 741.5'973--dc22

                    2009010528

 Summary: In a faraway kingdom, there lives an emperor who prizes fancy clothes
above all else. He buys suit after suit made of the most expensive materials instead
of tending to his threadbare kingdom. Then, one day, two traveling merchants offer
to make the emperor a special suit that has magical powers. The merchants, however,
 are not who they claim to be, and the suit has one major flaw — no one can see it!

Graphic Designer: Carla Zetina-Yglesias

Printed in the United States of America

HANS CHRISTIAN ANDERSON

The Emperor's New Clothes

THE GRAPHIC NOVEL

retold by
Stephanie True Peters

illustrated by
Jeffrey Stewart Timmins

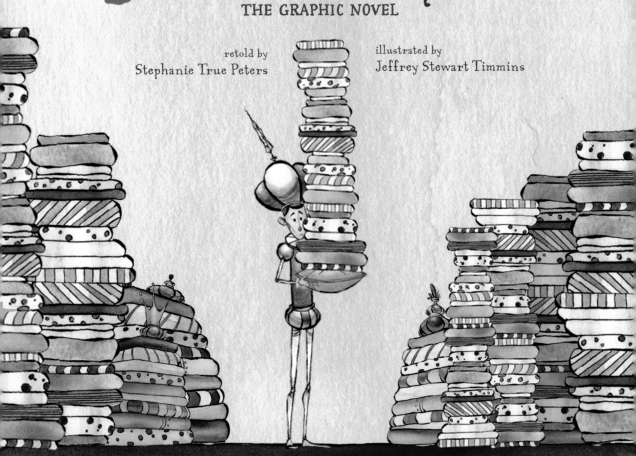

STONE ARCH BOOKS
MINNEAPOLIS   SAN DIEGO

Cast of Characters

THE SWINDLERS

THE TREASURER

THE BOY

THE EMPEROR

THE SERVANT

Rulers of other kingdoms inspected their soldiers.

Excellent! I've never seen a finer group in my life!

The emperor, however, inspected new hats.

Excellent! I've never seen a finer group in my life!

Other leaders ordered improvements to their kingdoms.

Shoes

Put a bridge there and spare no expense!

Very good, your Majesty!

3

Suddenly, something caught the emperor's eye.

Stop the carriage!

Two men were unrolling a beautiful bolt of cloth.

Make way! Make way!

The emperor was delighted with the cloth that he saw.

Such fine work! You are truly expert weavers!

Thank you, your Highness.

Yes, thank you.

TAP!
TAP!
TAP!

While the emperor waited, a frightful thought occurred to him.

Oh, no!

TAP!
TAP!

What if I'm not clever enough to see the magic cloth?

He peered inside to see . . .

. . . two weavers, two empty looms — and nothing more!

Your Highness, you are just in time!

As you can *clearly* see, we are done weaving!

Of course, the emperor couldn't see the cloth at all. But he knew better than to say so!

See how it shimmers!

So soft! So delicate!

It looks exactly like I imagined it! Begin my suit at once!

The weavers worked all day . . .

. . . and into the night.

Until at last, the emperor's new clothes were finished.

You look magnificent, Sire!

You simply must let everyone see you in your marvelous new suit!

Indeed! I shall hold a grand procession in the village tomorrow!

The emperor was quite pleased with the crowd's reaction.

HOORAY!

HOORAY!

HOORAY!

HOORAY!

HOORAY!

HOORAY!

HOORAY!

Until...

And the swindlers? They gave up their life of crime...

...at least until they spent all of the emperor's treasure!

Where to next, partner?

Wherever we can part a fool from his money!

glossary

ADORN (uh-DORN)—to decorate or add beauty to something

ATTIRE (uh-TIRE)—clothing

DELICATE (DEL-uh-kuht)—finely made and fragile

GARMENTS (GAR-muhntz)—pieces of clothing

INSISTED (in-SIST-id)—demanded something

INSPECTED (in-SPEKT-id)—looked at something very carefully

PROCESSION (pruh-SESH-uhn)—a number of people walking along as part of a parade

SHIMMERS (SHIM-urz)—shines with a faint, steady light

SIRE (SYE-ur)—a respectful term of address for a male ruler

SUBJECTS (SUHB-jiktz)—people who live in a kingdom under the rule of a king or queen

WARDROBE (WORD-robe)—a collection of clothes belonging to one person

about the author

Hans Christian Andersen was born in Odense, Denmark, on April 2, 1805. As Hans grew up, he tried many different professions, but none seemed to fit. He eventually found work as an actor and singer, but when his voice changed, he could no longer sing well enough to make a living. Then, a friend suggested that he start writing. A short time later, he published his first story, "The Ghost at Palnatoke's Grave."

Andersen's first book of fairy tales was published in 1835. He continued to write children's stories, publishing one almost every year, until he fell ill in 1872. Andersen had written more than 150 fairy tales before his death in 1875. He is considered to be the father of the modern fairy tale.

about the retelling author

After working more than 10 years as a children's book editor, Stephanie True Peters started writing books herself. She has since written 40 books, including the New York Times best seller *A Princess Primer: A Fairy Godmother's Guide to Being a Princess.* When not at her computer, Peters enjoys playing with her two children, hitting the gym, or working on home improvement projects with her patient and supportive husband, Daniel.

about the illustrator

Jeffrey Stewart Timmins was born July 2, 1979. In 2003, he graduated from the Classical Animation program at Sheridan College in Oakville, Ontario. He currently works as a freelance designer and animator. Even as an adult, Timmins still holds onto a few important items from his childhood, such as his rubber boots, cape, and lenseless sunglasses.

discussion questions

1. Why do you think it took so long for someone to point out that the emperor wasn't wearing any clothes?

2. Emperors are chosen by birth. Presidents are chosen by elections. Which way of choosing a leader do you think is better? Why?

3. If the Swindlers were caught, what do you think would be a fair punishment for them? Jail? A fine? Something else?

writing prompts

1. Imagine that you're an emperor. What kinds of laws would you make? Would you be a strict and stern ruler, or a kind and caring ruler? Write about your kingdom.

2. The Swindlers make money by tricking other people. Have you ever been tricked? What did you do about it? How did it make you feel?

3. At the end of the book, the Swindlers ran out of money. Do you think it was wise to spend it so quickly? What would you have done with all that wealth?

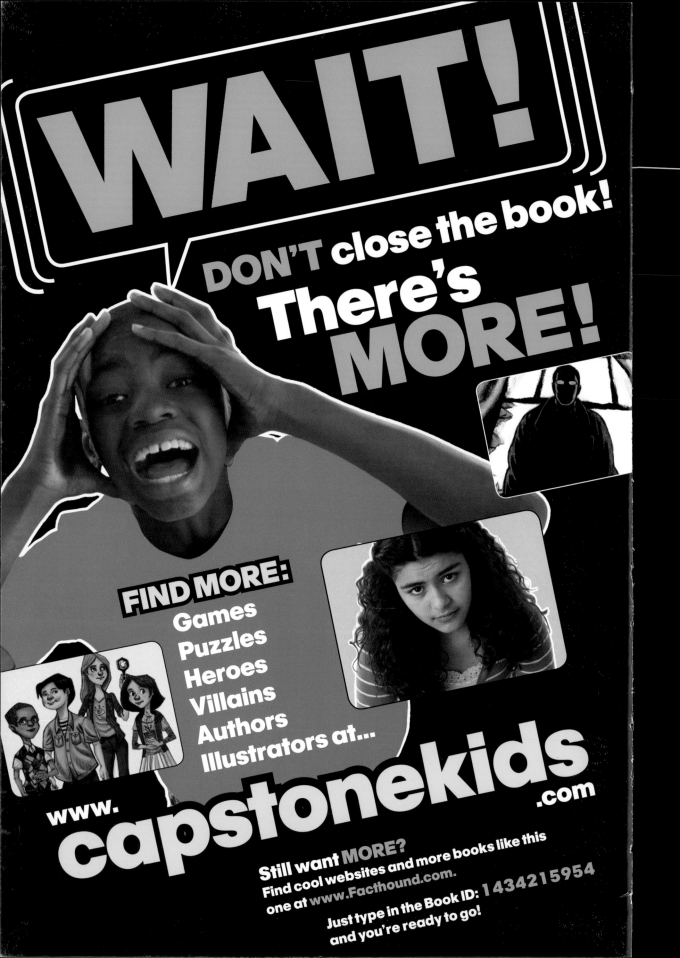